THE ENDLESS GAME

This is a work of fiction. Similarities to real people, places, or events are entirely coincidental.

THE ENDLESS GAME

First edition. November 12, 2024.

Copyright © 2024 Mortaza Tokhy.

ISBN: 979-8230618959

Written by Mortaza Tokhy.

Table of Contents

INTRODUCTION 1
CHAPTER 1 5
CHAPTER 2 23
CHAPTER 3 41
CHAPTER 4 57
CHAPTER 5 73
CHAPTER 6 87

In the sleepy suburban town of Oakridge, fourteen-year-old Mike Jensen lived an utterly average life - until the dusty attic of his family's home unveiled an ancient board game that would plunge him into a waking nightmare. "ChrotoQuest" seemed like an enticing relic from a bygone era when Mike discovered it, prompting him to invite his closest friends over for an innocent night of gaming and bonding. Little did they know the sinister forces they were toying with.

As the clock struck midnight, eerie sounds and blinding lights flooded Mike's bedroom, transporting the startled teens into a time loop prison of 24 repeating hours. Each cycle reset at the same haunting moment - Mike's best friend Jake vanishing into thin air at 3pm sharp. Trapped in this endless game, Mike became consumed with not just finding his lost companion, but unraveling the dark mysteries that tightened their grip with every loop.

A shadowy figure began appearing during certain cycles, seemingly observing and obstructing their efforts from the recesses of Mike's own attic. Scattered clues etched into the world around them hinted at hidden underground passages pulsing with secrets beneath Oakridge's streets. Paranoia festered as the group's trust eroded - could one of them be the true saboteur? Most harrowing were the time-bending consequences of their actions, where saving one life created new lethal threats, while failure ushered in grim fates worse than permanent deletion from existence itself.

Mike's dogged determination took him down an ever-darkening path. He uncovered that ChrotoQuest was actually an ancient game used to test the boundless potential of the human spirit - overseen by trans dimensional beings who could bend space, time, and reality on a whim. The only way to escape was to face a series of escalating trials designed to break his spirit and fracture his sanity.

With each cycle, the tasks grew more devious, from navigating treacherous mazes that remade themselves with each step, to combating personal demons manifested into physical form. Mike was forced to grapple with his deepest insecurities about growing up, the harsh realities of peer pressure, and a creeping sense of abandonment from his fractured family.

Only by mastering courage, loyalty, and self-acceptance could he overcome his greatest challenge - confronting the game's demented creator, an all-powerful being who could rewrite the universe on a whim. In a cosmic showdown that blurred all boundaries, Mike summoned every ounce of inner strength to out-maneuver his tormentor, reassembling the shattered shards of reality.

In a blinding rush, the time loops shattered and the game ended - but not before Mike made an agonizing sacrifice to liberate his best friend's soul. As the dust settled, he awakened on his bedroom floor, the real world finally restored but his life forever changed. Though Jake was gone, Mike carried profound new wisdom about the limitless power of the human spirit when challenged by the cruelest of injustices. ChrotoQuest had one final twist - proving that Mike's ordinary existence was merely one of infinite realities, and perhaps the grandest game of all.

CHAPTER 1

The Fateful Discovery

The dust swirls around me as I push aside another cardboard box, my fingers leaving trails in the thick grime coating everything in this forgotten attic. I've been up here for hours, searching for... something. Anything to break the monotony of another dreary Saturday.

My hand brushes against something solid, hidden beneath a moth-eaten blanket. "What have we here?" I mutter, carefully extricating a rectangular box from its resting place.

The word "ChrotoQuest" is etched in elegant gold script across the lid, which is intricately carved with swirling patterns that seem to shift before my eyes. My heart quickens as I trace the designs with my fingertip. This is no ordinary board game.

"Holy shit," I whisper, turning the box over in my hands. It's heavier than it looks, with a satisfying heft that speaks of quality craftsmanship. The wood is warm to the touch, almost pulsing with an energy I can't explain.

I pry open the lid, revealing a game board unlike anything I've ever seen. Concentric circles of gleaming metal, inlaid with strange symbols and miniature clockwork gears. Game pieces that look like they're carved from crystal, catching the dim light filtering through the dusty attic window.

My mind races with possibilities. Where did this come from? How long has it been hidden up here? And most importantly - how the hell do you play it?

Tucking the game securely under my arm, I scramble down the rickety attic stairs, nearly tripping in my excitement. I have to show this to the guys. This is too good to keep to myself.

I grab my phone, fingers flying as I text our group chat:

"Guys, you won't believe what I just found. Get over here ASAP. Game night's about to get wild."

Jake's the first to respond: "Dude, it's barely noon. What's got you so worked up?"

I snap a quick photo of the game and send it. "Trust me, you're gonna want to see this in person."

One by one, they all chime in, promising to be over within the hour. A thrill runs through me as I imagine us gathered around this mysterious game, unraveling its secrets together. For the first time in months, I feel a spark of genuine excitement.

As I wait for my friends to arrive, I can't stop examining the game, running my fingers over its smooth surface. There's something... different about it. Something that makes the hair on the back of my neck stand up, even as my heart races with anticipation.

Whatever happens tonight, I have a feeling our lives are about to change. And honestly? I can't wait.

The doorbell chimes, jolting me from my reverie. I bound down the stairs, yanking the door open to reveal Jake's grinning face.

"Alright, Jensen, what's this big mystery you've got us all worked up about?" he asks, stepping inside.

I'm about to answer when Sarah's beat-up Chevy pulls up, Alex in the passenger seat. "Hold that thought," I tell Jake.

As Sarah and Alex join us, the energy in the room crackles. Sarah's eyes are bright with curiosity, while Alex's calm demeanor barely masks his excitement.

"So, are you going to keep us in suspense all night?" Sarah teases, playfully nudging my arm.

I can't help but grin. "Follow me, you impatient lot."

As we climb the stairs to my room, I feel a mix of excitement and... something else. A faint unease I can't quite place.

"I swear, Mike, if this is another one of your elaborate pranks..." Alex starts.

"It's not, I promise," I assure him, pushing open my bedroom door.

The game sits on my bed, bathed in the soft glow of my desk lamp. The room feels different somehow, shadows deeper than usual.

"Whoa," Jake breathes, moving closer to inspect the game. "Where'd you find this?"

"Attic," I reply, watching their reactions closely. "Pretty cool, right?"

Sarah runs her fingers over the intricate carvings on the board. "It's beautiful," she murmurs. "But also... kind of creepy?"

I nod, relieved I'm not the only one feeling it. "Yeah, there's definitely something... different about it."

Alex, ever the voice of reason, asks, "Are you sure it's safe to play? It looks ancient."

I hesitate, that nagging sense of unease growing stronger. But the pull of the game is irresistible. "Only one way to find out, right?"

As we gather around, the excitement in the room is palpable, tinged with a hint of apprehension. The lamp flickers, casting dancing shadows on the walls.

I catch Sarah's eye, and she gives me a small, nervous smile. "Well," she says, "let's see what this ChrotoQuest is all about."

My heart races as I reach for the rulebook. Whatever happens next, I have a feeling our lives will never be the same.

I open the rulebook, its pages yellowed and brittle. "Okay, let's see... 'ChrotoQuest: A Journey Through Time and Peril,'" I read aloud, my voice shakier than I'd like.

Jake leans in, peering at the intricate game pieces. "Cool, we each get a character token. Dibs on the warrior!"

Sarah giggles, but it sounds forced. "Of course you do. I'll take the... sorceress, I guess?"

As I continue reading, the rules become increasingly bizarre. "Guys, listen to this: 'Beware the shadows that lengthen, for time is not your ally.' What does that even mean?"

Alex frowns, adjusting his glasses. "Probably just atmospheric nonsense. Right?"

I nod, not entirely convinced. "Yeah, must be."

We set up the board, our laughter growing more nervous with each passing minute. The game's design is unlike anything I've seen – shifting pathways, cryptic symbols, and a central clock with thirteen hours.

"Thirteen?" Sarah whispers. "That can't be good."

I glance at my bedside clock. 11:45 PM. A chill runs down my spine.

"Maybe we should wait until tomorrow," I suggest, suddenly hesitant.

Jake scoffs. "Come on, Mike! Where's your sense of adventure?"

I look around at my friends, their faces a mix of excitement and unease. Despite the growing knot in my stomach, I can't bring myself to disappoint them.

"Alright," I concede. "Let's do this."

As we prepare to start, I can't shake the feeling that the shadows in my room are deepening, creeping closer. The air grows colder, and the ticking of my clock seems impossibly loud.

Sarah shivers. "Is it just me, or did it get freezing in here?"

I wrap my arms around myself, trying to calm my racing heart. "Yeah, it's... weird."

The minute hand inches towards midnight, and I swear I can feel the game thrumming with energy. We exchange nervous glances, all pretense of casual fun evaporating.

"Last chance to back out," Alex murmurs.

I take a deep breath, my hand hovering over the dice. "No, we're in this together. Whatever happens... we face it as a team."

The clock strikes midnight.

The moment the clock strikes twelve, all hell breaks loose. A deafening, otherworldly screech pierces the air, making us all clamp our hands over our ears. The board game erupts in a blinding flash of light, so intense I have to squeeze my eyes shut.

"What's happening?" I yell, but my voice is drowned out by the cacophony of sound and light assaulting us.

I feel a violent lurch, as if the entire room is spinning. My stomach drops like I'm on a roller coaster plummeting from its highest peak. When I manage to pry my eyes open, I'm met with a kaleidoscope of swirling colors and fractured images.

"Guys?" I call out, panic rising in my throat. "Where are you?"

Sarah's terrified scream cuts through the chaos. "Mike! I can't see anything!"

I try to move towards her voice, but my limbs feel heavy, like I'm wading through molasses. "Hold on! I'm coming!"

Suddenly, everything stops. The noise cuts out abruptly, plunging us into an eerie silence. The lights fade, leaving us in near-total darkness. As my eyes adjust, I realize we're still in my bedroom, but something feels... off.

"Is everyone okay?" I ask, my voice shaky.

"I think so," Jake replies, sounding dazed. "What the hell just happened?"

Before I can answer, my alarm clock starts blaring. I fumble for it, confused. When I finally manage to shut it off, I freeze, staring at the display in disbelief.

"Guys," I whisper, "it's midnight again."

Alex laughs nervously. "Very funny, Mike. Your clock must be broken."

But as we look around, we notice other details. The game is back in its starting position. Our snacks are untouched. Even the positions we're sitting in – they're exactly how we were when we first started playing.

"This isn't possible," Sarah murmurs, her face pale in the dim light.

A horrible realization dawns on me. "I think... I think we're trapped in some kind of time loop."

The room falls silent as the implications of my words sink in. I can see the fear and confusion mirrored in my friends' faces, matching the churning anxiety in my gut.

"What do we do now?" Jake asks, his usual bravado nowhere to be found.

I swallow hard, trying to keep my voice steady. "I don't know. But we need to figure this out. Fast."

As we huddle together, the game board seems to loom in the center of our circle, its intricate designs now looking less like a game and more like a sinister trap. And as the clock ticks forward, I can't shake the feeling that our ordeal is only just beginning.

The hours crawl by, each minute feeling like an eternity as we grapple with our impossible situation. We've been talking in circles, trying to make sense of it all, when suddenly the air in the room shifts. It's 2:59 PM.

"Guys, I don't feel so good," Jake mumbles, his face ashen.

I reach out to steady him. "Jake, what's wrong?"

The clock strikes 3:00 PM.

In an instant, Jake vanishes. One moment he's there, solid beneath my hand, and the next – nothing. Just empty air.

"Jake!" I scream, my heart pounding so hard I think it might burst from my chest. "Jake, where are you?"

Sarah jumps to her feet, knocking over a lamp in her panic. "What just happened? Where did he go?"

"This isn't funny, Jake!" Alex shouts, his voice cracking. "Come out, man!"

I'm on my hands and knees, frantically searching under the bed, in the closet, anywhere Jake could possibly be hiding. But deep down, I know it's futile. He's gone.

"We have to find him," I say, my voice barely above a whisper. "We can't... we can't lose him."

For the next few hours, we tear the house apart. We call Jake's phone repeatedly, but it just rings in his abandoned backpack. As the sun begins to set, we collapse in exhausted heaps in my living room.

"What if he's gone for good?" Sarah asks, her eyes red-rimmed from crying.

I shake my head vehemently. "No, we can't think like that. He has to be somewhere."

Alex runs his hands through his hair, tugging at the roots. "But where, Mike? We've looked everywhere. It's like he just... ceased to exist."

"Maybe..." I start, the idea forming as I speak, "Maybe this is part of the game. The time loop, Jake disappearing – it's all connected."

Sarah leans forward, her brow furrowed. "You think the game is doing this? But how?"

"I don't know," I admit. "But think about it. We start playing this weird, old game, and suddenly we're stuck in a time loop? It can't be a coincidence."

Alex nods slowly. "Okay, so if it is the game, how do we stop it? How do we get Jake back?"

I glance at the clock – 11:45 PM. "We've got fifteen minutes until the day resets. We need to figure out the rules of this... whatever it is we're trapped in."

As we huddle together, throwing out theories and possibilities, I can feel the tension building. Sarah keeps glancing at Alex suspiciously, as if he might be the next to vanish. Alex, in turn, seems to be inching away from both of us.

"What if..." Sarah begins, then stops, biting her lip.

"What?" I prompt.

She takes a deep breath. "What if one of us made Jake disappear? What if it's not the game, but one of us?"

The accusation hangs in the air, heavy and poisonous. I want to deny it immediately, but a small part of me wonders – could she be right?

As the clock ticks closer to midnight, I can feel our friendship fraying at the edges. The trust we've built over years is being tested in ways I never imagined possible. And as the familiar eerie sounds begin to fill the air, signaling another reset, I'm left wondering – will we be able to save Jake and ourselves before it's too late?

The sound of creaking floorboards draws my attention to the attic entrance. My heart nearly stops as I catch a glimpse of a dark, shadowy figure lurking in the doorway. It's there for just a moment, observing us with an intensity I can feel even from across the room, before it melts back into the darkness.

"Did you see that?" I whisper, my voice barely audible.

Sarah and Alex exchange confused glances. "See what?" Alex asks, his brow furrowed.

I shake my head, unsure if I should mention it. The tension between us is already thick enough to cut with a knife. "Nothing," I mutter, but I can't shake the feeling of being watched.

As the days – or rather, the same day – continue to repeat, I find myself growing more determined with each reset. Jake's absence is a constant ache, a reminder of my failure to protect my friends.

"We're going to figure this out," I announce, pacing the room as Sarah and Alex watch me warily. "We need to be methodical. Document everything that happens, no matter how small."

"And what if we can't?" Sarah's voice is small, defeated. "What if we're stuck here forever?"

I kneel in front of her, meeting her eyes. "We won't be. I promise you, I'm going to get us out of this. All of us, including Jake."

Alex scoffs. "Big words, Mike. But how exactly do you plan on doing that?"

I stand, squaring my shoulders. "By taking charge. No more sitting around waiting for something to happen. We're going to make it happen."

As I outline my plan – exploring every inch of the house, testing the boundaries of our prison, trying to communicate with whatever force is behind this – I can feel a shift in the room. The weight of leadership settles on my shoulders, heavy but not unwelcome.

"What about the attic?" I ask, my eyes darting to the doorway where I saw the figure. "We need to search it thoroughly."

Sarah shudders. "I don't like it up there. It feels... wrong."

"I know," I say softly, placing a hand on her shoulder. "But we have to. For Jake."

As we prepare to venture into the attic, I can't shake the feeling that we're being watched. The shadowy figure lingers in my mind, a constant reminder of the danger we're in. But with each passing cycle, my resolve only grows stronger. We will break free from this loop, we will find Jake, and we will survive – together.

I sink onto the edge of my bed, the springs creaking under my weight. The room feels different now – claustrophobic, almost alive with an unseen energy. My friends' faces are etched with worry, their eyes constantly darting to the shadows.

"Guys," I say, breaking the tense silence. "I need a minute. Can you...?"

They nod, filing out quietly. As the door clicks shut, I let out a long, shaky breath.

"What have I gotten us into?" I whisper, running my hands through my hair.

The gravity of our situation hits me like a ton of bricks. We're trapped in a time loop, Jake is missing, and there's something sinister lurking in the attic. And somehow, I've become the de facto leader of this nightmare.

I close my eyes, trying to center myself. "Think, Mike. Think."

The image of the board game flashes in my mind. ChrotoQuest. It all started with that damned game.

"There has to be a connection," I mutter, pacing the room. "The game, the time loop, Jake's disappearance. It's all linked somehow."

I stop at the window, staring out at the unchanging streetscape. It's always the same time, always the same scene. But there has to be a way to break the cycle.

"We're missing something," I say to my reflection. "Some clue, some rule we haven't figured out yet."

A chill runs down my spine as I remember the shadowy figure in the attic. Is it watching us even now? Is it the key to our escape or the source of our imprisonment?

I turn back to face the room, my jaw set with determination. "Whatever it takes, we're going to solve this puzzle. We're going to get Jake back, and we're going to get out of here."

As I reach for the doorknob to rejoin my friends, I pause. The weight of responsibility settles heavily on my shoulders, but with it comes a surge of resolve.

"No matter what happens," I vow to the empty room, "I will not let them down."

CHAPTER 2

Unraveling the Loop

I stared at the faces of my friends, huddled in my dimly lit bedroom. The air felt thick with tension, our usual laughter replaced by an uneasy silence. Jake's empty spot on the beanbag chair seemed to mock us, a stark reminder of the inexplicable events we'd just experienced.

"Guys, we need to figure this out," I said, breaking the silence. My voice sounded strange, even to me. "Let's retrace our steps. What exactly happened before Jake vanished?"

Sarah hugged her knees to her chest, her eyes wide. "We were playing ChrotoQuest, and then... poof. He was gone."

"It doesn't make any sense," Alex muttered, running a hand through his messy hair. "People don't just disappear."

I could feel their eyes on me, waiting for answers I didn't have. The weight of leadership settled on my shoulders, heavy and uncomfortable. "Okay, let's break it down. What do we know about ChrotoQuest?"

"It's just a game," Alex said, his tone skeptical. "A bunch of code and graphics. It can't actually affect reality."

But even as he spoke, I could see the doubt in his eyes. None of us wanted to admit the possibility that something beyond our understanding was at play.

"What if it's not just a game?" Lily's soft voice cut through the room. She'd been quiet until now, her artistic mind no doubt piecing together the puzzle. "What if it's some kind of... portal?"

I felt a chill run down my spine at her words. It sounded crazy, but after what we'd seen, could we really rule anything out?

"A portal?" Sarah scoffed, but I could hear the tremor in her voice. "To where? Another dimension?"

"Or another time," I found myself saying. The words hung in the air, heavy with implication.

Alex shook his head vigorously. "No way. Time travel isn't real. There has to be a logical explanation."

THE ENDLESS GAME

As they argued, my mind raced. I thought about the game's intricate design, the way it seemed to anticipate our moves. Had we unknowingly triggered something when we started playing?

"What if," I began, my thoughts coalescing, "what if ChrotoQuest is more than just a game? What if it's some kind of... test?"

The room fell silent as my friends considered this. I could almost see the gears turning in their heads, each of them grappling with the impossible situation we found ourselves in.

"A test for what?" Lily asked, her eyes shining with a mix of fear and curiosity.

I shook my head, frustration building. "I don't know. But we need to figure it out. For Jake's sake."

As I looked at my friends' worried faces, I knew we were in this together. Whatever was happening, whatever ChrotoQuest really was, we would unravel its mysteries. We had to. Jake's life might depend on it.

I glanced at my watch. 2:45 PM. Fifteen minutes until Jake's disappearance. My heart raced as I laid out our plan.

"Okay, here's what we're going to do," I said, trying to keep my voice steady. "We'll form a human chain around Jake. Alex, you take his left arm. Sarah, his right. Lily and I will stand behind and in front of him."

Jake's face was pale, but he nodded. "You really think this will work?"

I swallowed hard. "It has to."

We moved into position, our bodies tense. The air felt thick with anticipation. I could hear everyone's shallow breathing, see the sweat beading on Jake's forehead.

"Two minutes," Sarah whispered.

My mind raced. What if this didn't work? What if Jake slipped through our grasp like smoke? I pushed the thoughts away, focusing on the warmth of Jake's shoulder beneath my hand.

"One minute," Alex called out, his voice cracking.

Jake's eyes met mine, filled with a mix of hope and terror. "Mike, if this doesn't work-"

"It will," I cut him off, more forcefully than I intended. "It has to."

The second hand on my watch ticked relentlessly. Ten seconds. Five. Three. Two. One.

A flash of light erupted between us, blinding and disorienting. I felt Jake's presence vanish, my hands grasping at empty air.

"No!" I yelled, blinking furiously to clear my vision. "Jake!"

As the spots faded from my eyes, I saw my friends stumbling back, their faces etched with shock and despair. The space where Jake had stood was empty.

"I can't believe it," Lily whispered, her voice breaking. "He's gone. Again."

I felt a wave of helplessness wash over me. We had planned so carefully, tried so hard, and yet Jake had vanished as if we'd done nothing at all.

"What now?" Sarah asked, her usual confidence shattered. "If this didn't work, what will?"

I ran my hands through my hair, fighting back tears of frustration. "I don't know," I admitted. "I just... I don't know."

The weight of our failure settled over us like a heavy blanket. We had been so sure, so certain that our plan would work. Now, faced with Jake's absence once again, I felt utterly lost.

"We can't give up," I said finally, more to convince myself than anyone else. "There has to be something we're missing. Some clue we've overlooked."

But as I looked at my friends' defeated expressions, I wondered if we were truly in over our heads. How could we fight against something we couldn't even understand?

As we stood there, grappling with our failure, a flicker of movement caught my eye. I jerked my head towards the corner of the room, heart suddenly racing.

"Did you see that?" I whispered, afraid to speak too loudly.

Sarah frowned. "See what?"

I squinted, trying to focus on the shadowy area near my closet. For a split second, I could have sworn I saw... something. A dark shape, barely there and then gone.

"I... I'm not sure," I said, uncertainty creeping into my voice. "It was like a shadow, but... moving on its own."

Lily's eyes widened. "You don't think it's... connected to Jake's disappearance, do you?"

I shook my head, trying to clear it. "I don't know. Maybe I'm just seeing things."

But as we gathered again the next day, that fleeting glimpse haunted me. We huddled in my room, the atmosphere thick with tension and unspoken fears.

"Okay," I began, trying to sound more confident than I felt. "We need to come up with a new plan. Any ideas?"

Sarah leaned forward, her brow furrowed. "What about that shadow you saw? Could it be important?"

I hesitated. "I'm not sure. It was so quick, I can't be certain I really saw anything."

"But what if it wasn't just your imagination?" Lily interjected, her voice trembling slightly. "What if there's... something else involved in all this?"

The room fell silent as we all considered the implications. The idea that some unknown entity might be behind Jake's disappearances sent a chill down my spine.

"Friend or foe?" I mused aloud, more to myself than the others.

"How can you even ask that?" Sarah snapped, her eyes flashing. "If it's responsible for Jake vanishing, it can't be friendly!"

I held up my hands defensively. "I'm just trying to consider all possibilities. We can't afford to make assumptions."

But as I looked at my friends' faces, I could see the paranoia setting in. The shadow, whether real or imagined, had added a new layer of fear to our already desperate situation.

I took a deep breath, pushing back against the creeping dread. "Look, we need to focus. There's got to be something we're missing." My eyes drifted to the ceiling, and suddenly an idea struck. "The attic. We haven't checked the attic yet."

Sarah's eyebrows shot up. "The attic? Why would there be anything up there?"

"I don't know," I admitted, "but it's worth a shot. This house is old, who knows what secrets it might be hiding?"

Reluctantly, the others agreed. We made our way to the narrow staircase leading up to the attic, the old wood creaking ominously beneath our feet. As I pushed open the hatch, a wave of musty air washed over us.

"God, it smells like my great-aunt's closet up here," Lily muttered, wrinkling her nose.

I pulled the cord for the single bare bulb, casting long shadows across the cramped space. Dust motes danced in the weak light, and cobwebs clung to every corner. But it wasn't the grime that caught my attention – it was the walls.

"Holy shit," I breathed, my eyes widening. "Look at this."

Etched into the weathered wood paneling were strange symbols, unlike anything I'd ever seen before. Circles intersecting with jagged lines, spirals that seemed to twist into infinity, and shapes that hurt my eyes if I stared too long.

"What...what are they?" Sarah whispered, her earlier skepticism replaced by awe.

I ran my fingers over the nearest marking, feeling the rough grooves beneath my skin. "I have no idea. But they're old. Really old."

As we spread out, examining the bizarre etchings, a chill ran down my spine. There was something deeply unsettling about these symbols, as if they were trying to convey a message I couldn't quite grasp.

"Guys," Lily's voice quavered from across the attic. "I think I found something else."

We hurried over to where she was crouched by a section of floorboard. Her fingers were tracing the edge of what looked like a hidden compartment.

"Help me lift this," I said, kneeling beside her.

Together, we pried up the loose board, revealing a small space beneath. And there, nestled in the darkness, was a rolled-up piece of paper.

With trembling hands, I carefully unrolled it. "It's... it's a map," I said, my voice barely above a whisper.

The others crowded around, their breath hot on my neck as we stared at the faded document. It showed an intricate network of tunnels and chambers, all seemingly running beneath the very ground of Oakridge.

"Underground passages," Sarah murmured, a mix of excitement and fear in her voice. "But why? And how did they get here?"

I shook my head, my mind reeling with possibilities. "I don't know. But I think we just found our next lead."

As we huddled there in the dim attic, surrounded by those eerie symbols and clutching this unexpected treasure map, I felt a surge of hope mingled with dread. We were one step closer to solving the mystery – but I couldn't shake the feeling that we were also diving headfirst into something far more dangerous than we could imagine.

I rolled up the map and turned to face my friends. The excitement of our discovery quickly faded as I saw the apprehension etched on their faces.

"We have to explore those passages," I said, my voice firm. "It's our best lead to figuring out what's happening to Jake."

Sarah's eyes widened. "Are you crazy, Mike? We don't know what's down there. It could be dangerous!"

"Exactly," Tom chimed in, crossing his arms. "We're not spelunkers. What if we get lost? Or worse?"

I felt my frustration rising. "So we just give up? Let Jake disappear over and over again?"

"No one's saying that," Lisa interjected, her voice soft but resolute. "But we need to think this through. Maybe we should tell the adults, get some help."

I scoffed. "And say what? That we found a secret map in the attic while trying to solve a magical time loop? They'll think we're nuts."

The tension in the room was palpable. I could see the doubt creeping into their eyes, the trust we'd built starting to crack under the weight of our fear.

"Look," I said, trying to keep my voice steady. "I know it's scary. But we're in this together. We can't back out now."

Tom shook his head. "I don't know, Mike. This is getting too intense. Maybe... maybe we should step back, try to find another way."

I felt a lump forming in my throat. These were my best friends, and I was asking them to follow me into the unknown. The weight of leadership suddenly felt crushing.

"I need some air," I muttered, pushing past them and heading for the attic stairs. I couldn't bear to see the doubt in their eyes any longer.

Outside, I leaned against the cool brick of the house, taking deep breaths. The afternoon sun felt too bright, too normal for the madness we were living through. I closed my eyes, trying to steady myself.

What if I was wrong? What if I was leading my friends into danger? The thought of losing them, of being responsible for their harm, made my stomach churn. But then Jake's face flashed in my mind, his expression of terror as he vanished before our eyes.

I clenched my fists. No, we had to keep going. We had to solve this, no matter what. I couldn't let fear stop us now.

"I won't let you down," I whispered, to Jake, to my friends, to myself. "We're going to figure this out. Whatever it takes."

With renewed determination, I straightened up, ready to face my friends again. We'd come too far to turn back now. Whatever lay in those underground passages, we'd face it together.

I took a deep breath and headed back inside, my mind racing with plans. As I entered the attic, my friends' voices hushed. Their eyes locked onto me, a mix of uncertainty and expectation in their gazes.

"Alright," I said, my voice steadier than I felt. "We're doing this. Those passages might be our only lead to saving Jake."

Sarah nodded, her earlier skepticism replaced by determination. "What's the plan, Mike?"

I laid out a makeshift map on the dusty floor. "We'll need flashlights, rope, and maybe some food. Who knows how long we'll be down there."

"I've got some power banks for our phones," Alex chimed in, already rummaging through his backpack.

As we gathered supplies, the urgency in the air was palpable. Every tick of the clock seemed to echo Jake's absence.

"Remember," I cautioned, "we stick together. No wandering off alone."

We were nearly ready when I saw it - a flicker of movement in the corner of my eye. I whipped around, heart pounding.

"Guys," I whispered, "did you-"

The shadowy figure was there and gone in an instant, like smoke dissipating. A chill ran down my spine.

"I saw it too," Sarah breathed, her face pale.

We exchanged glances, fear and resolve battling in our expressions. The presence of the figure only confirmed our suspicions - there was more to this mystery than we knew.

"Let's go," I said, my voice low but firm. "Whatever's down there, we face it together."

As we filed out of the attic, I couldn't shake the feeling we were being watched. But there was no turning back now. Our adventure into the unknown had begun, and Jake's fate hung in the balance.

I stood at the mouth of the tunnel, my flashlight beam cutting through the inky darkness ahead. The air was thick with the smell of damp earth and something else I couldn't quite place. My friends huddled close behind me, their breaths shallow and quick.

"Well," I said, trying to keep my voice steady, "this is it. Our ticket to answers... or more questions."

Sarah's hand found mine in the darkness. "Mike, are you sure about this? We don't know what's down there."

I squeezed her hand, grateful for the connection. "No, we don't. But Jake's counting on us. We can't back out now."

Alex peered over my shoulder, his usual bravado notably absent. "It's just... so dark. Like it could swallow us whole."

I nodded, understanding his fear all too well. "That's why we stick together. No matter what."

Taking a deep breath, I took my first step into the passage. The ground beneath my feet was uneven, slick with moisture. I heard the others fall in line behind me, our footsteps echoing off the narrow walls.

"Keep your eyes peeled for any of those symbols we saw in the attic," I reminded them. "They might be our only clue to navigating this maze."

As we ventured deeper, the world above seemed to fade away. The darkness pressed in from all sides, our flashlights creating islands of light in a sea of black. I couldn't shake the feeling that we were being watched, that something was waiting for us in the depths.

"Hey, Mike?" Alex's voice was barely above a whisper. "What if we can't find our way back?"

I paused, turning to face my friends. Their faces were etched with worry in the harsh light of our flashlights. "We will," I assured them, even as doubt gnawed at my insides. "We have to. For Jake."

With one last look at the fading light of the entrance behind us, we pressed on into the unknown. Whatever challenges lay ahead, we'd face them together. The fate of our friend – and perhaps the entire town – rested on our shoulders.

CHAPTER 3

The Consequences of Time

The air in my bedroom feels heavy, like it's pressing down on all of us. I glance around at my friends' faces, illuminated by the soft glow of my desk lamp. Sarah's biting her lower lip, a nervous habit she's had since we were kids. Tom's pacing back and forth, his fingers drumming an erratic rhythm against his thigh. And Jake... Jake's just staring blankly at the wall, his usual easygoing smile nowhere to be seen.

"We can't keep doing this," Sarah finally breaks the silence, her voice barely above a whisper. "It's tearing us apart."

I nod, feeling the weight of her words. We've been through so many loops now, each one more devastating than the last. The exhaustion is etched into every line of our faces, the frustration simmering just beneath the surface.

Tom stops pacing abruptly, turning to face us. "But we can't give up. There has to be a way out of this... this nightmare."

I want to agree with him, to believe there's still hope, but the memory of our last attempt floods my mind. "Guys," I start, my throat tight, "we need to talk about what happened in the last loop."

Jake flinches visibly, and I know he's reliving it too. The silence stretches on, oppressive and suffocating.

"We tried to save Jake," Sarah says softly, her eyes glistening with unshed tears. "We thought... we thought we had it all figured out."

"But instead," Tom continues, his voice cracking, "we ended up getting Emily hurt. How could we have known that pushing Jake out of the way of that car would-"

"Would cause Emily to get hit instead?" Jake finishes, his words laced with bitterness. "God, I can still hear her scream."

The room falls silent again as we all remember the sickening crunch of metal on flesh, the way Emily's body had crumpled like a rag doll. My stomach churns at the memory.

"I don't understand," I murmur, more to myself than to the others. "We were so careful. We planned everything out. How could it have gone so wrong?"

Sarah shakes her head, her fingers twisting anxiously in her lap. "It's like the game is actively working against us. Like it's... changing the rules."

"Or maybe we just don't understand the rules at all," Tom suggests, running a hand through his disheveled hair.

I feel a chill run down my spine at his words. What if he's right? What if we've been fumbling in the dark this whole time, thinking we're making progress when we're really just digging ourselves deeper?

"So what do we do now?" Jake asks, his voice small and vulnerable in a way I've never heard before. "How do we keep going when every move we make seems to hurt someone?"

I wish I had an answer for him, for all of us. But as I look around at my friends' defeated expressions, I realize that we're all just as lost and scared as each other. And for the first time since this nightmare began, I'm not sure if we'll ever find our way out.

The weight of responsibility settles on my shoulders like a lead blanket. I can feel everyone's eyes on me, waiting for answers I don't have. My mind races, desperately trying to piece together the fragments of information we've gathered across the loops.

"There has to be a pattern," I think, my brow furrowing. "Some kind of logic to this twisted game. If we could just figure out the rules..."

But even as I try to convince myself, fear gnaws at the edges of my resolve. What if there are no rules? What if we're just pawns in some cruel, cosmic joke?

I shake my head, pushing the thought away. No. We can't give up. We have to keep fighting, keep trying to understand.

"Okay," I say, breaking the heavy silence. "We need to think about this logically. What do we know for sure?"

Sarah sits up straighter, her analytical mind kicking into gear. "We know the loops reset every 24 hours. And we know our actions have consequences, even if we can't always predict them."

"But how do we know which actions to take?" Tom interjects, frustration evident in his voice. "Every time we try to help, we end up making things worse!"

Jake nods in agreement. "Maybe we should just... stop trying. Stay put and wait it out."

"We can't do that!" I argue, feeling a surge of determination. "We have to keep trying. There has to be a way out of this."

"And risk hurting more people?" Sarah counters, her eyes flashing. "Mike, we almost got Emily killed last time!"

The tension in the room ratchets up a notch. I can feel our friendships straining under the weight of our disagreements.

"So what, we just give up?" I snap, anger and fear making my voice sharp. "Let this thing win?"

Tom stands up, pacing the small confines of my bedroom. "Maybe Jake's right. Maybe doing nothing is better than doing the wrong thing."

I feel a surge of betrayal at his words. "I can't believe you're all willing to just roll over and accept this!"

"We're not accepting it," Sarah says, her voice tight with emotion. "We're just... we're scared, Mike. We don't want to make things worse."

I look around at my friends, seeing the fear and uncertainty in their eyes. And suddenly, I feel ashamed of my outburst. They're right to be afraid. We all are.

"I'm sorry," I say softly, deflating. "I'm scared too. But I can't... I can't just do nothing. There has to be a way out, and I'm going to find it. Even if I have to do it alone."

The silence that follows is heavy with unspoken words and fraying bonds of friendship. And I wonder, not for the first time, if we'll ever be the same after this.

As I look at my friends' worried faces, something clicks in my mind. A memory surfaces, hazy at first, but growing clearer with each passing second. My heart starts to race.

"Wait," I say, my voice barely above a whisper. "I think... I think I remember something from a previous loop."

Sarah leans forward, her eyes wide. "What is it, Mike?"

I close my eyes, trying to grasp the elusive memory. "There was... a voice. I couldn't see who was speaking, but I heard it clearly. It said, 'Only through trials shall you break free.'"

My eyes snap open, and I can feel a mix of excitement and apprehension coursing through me. "Don't you see? We're not just stuck in a loop. We're being tested. There are trials we have to face!"

Tom's brow furrows. "Trials? What kind of trials?"

I shake my head. "I don't know, but it's something. It's a lead we didn't have before."

Jake scoffs, but I can see a glimmer of interest in his eyes. "And how do we know these 'trials' won't just make things worse?"

"We don't," I admit. "But it's the first real clue we've had about how to break this cycle."

Sarah bites her lip, looking thoughtful. "It... it does make a weird kind of sense. Like we're in some twisted game."

I watch as the information sinks in, gauging their reactions. Tom looks skeptical but intrigued, his analytical mind clearly working overtime. Sarah seems cautiously optimistic, her natural curiosity piqued. Jake, ever the pessimist, still looks doubtful, but I can see the wheels turning in his head.

"Look," I say, "I know it's scary. But if we work together, face these trials as a team, we might have a chance. We can't keep living the same day over and over. We have to try something."

There's a moment of silence as they process this. Then, to my surprise, it's Jake who speaks up.

"I still think this is crazy," he says, his voice gruff. "But... you're right. We can't keep doing nothing. If there are trials, let's face them. Together."

I feel a surge of hope as Tom and Sarah nod in agreement. We're scared, we're uncertain, but for the first time in what feels like forever, we have a purpose. A direction.

As I look at my friends, I realize that whatever these trials might be, we'll face them as one. And maybe, just maybe, that will be enough to break us free from this nightmare.

As I look at my friends' determined faces, a memory suddenly resurfaces, hitting me like a jolt of electricity. My mind whirls back to a previous loop, the attic, the shadowy figure...

The musty smell of old wood and dust fills my nostrils. I'm standing at the top of the attic stairs, heart pounding, sweat beading on my forehead. The dim light from my flashlight barely penetrates the gloom, casting eerie shadows across the cluttered space.

And then I see it. A figure, darker than the surrounding shadows, looming in the far corner. It's tall, impossibly tall, with limbs that seem too long and too thin to be human. I can't make out any features, just a void where a face should be.

"Who... what are you?" I manage to stammer out.

The figure doesn't move, doesn't speak. But somehow, I hear words in my mind, cold and ancient: "The trials await. Prove yourselves worthy."

I blink, and I'm back in my bedroom, staring at my friends. They're looking at me with concern.

"Mike? You okay?" Sarah asks, her brow furrowed.

I take a deep breath. "Yeah, I... I just remembered something. From a previous loop. I think I know where we need to go next."

Tom leans forward, his eyes bright with curiosity. "Where?"

"The attic," I say, my voice steadier than I feel. "I saw something up there once. I think it's connected to these trials."

Jake scoffs, crossing his arms. "The attic? Seriously? What, you think there's some magical portal up there or something?"

"I don't know what's up there," I admit. "But I know it's important. We need to explore it further."

Sarah nods slowly. "It's worth a shot. We've tried everything else."

Tom stands up, already heading for the door. "Let's do it. Anything's better than sitting around waiting for the day to reset."

But Jake hesitates, fear flashing across his face. "What if... what if we find something we can't handle? What if we make things worse?"

I meet his gaze, understanding his fear all too well. "We stick together. Whatever's up there, we face it as a team. Okay?"

After a moment, Jake nods, his jaw set with determination. "Okay. Let's do this."

As we head for the attic stairs, I can't shake the memory of that shadowy figure. Whatever trials await us, I have a feeling they're going to push us to our limits. But as I look at my friends, I know we're ready to face whatever comes our way.

The ancient wooden stairs groan under our weight as we ascend, each creak echoing in the stillness. My heart pounds, a staccato rhythm matching our cautious steps. The air grows thicker, dustier, with each floor we climb.

"Anyone else feel like we're walking into a horror movie?" Tom whispers, his usual bravado wavering.

I swallow hard, my throat dry. "Just stay close," I murmur, leading the way.

The dim light from my phone casts eerie shadows on the walls, transforming familiar corners into menacing shapes. Sarah's breath hitches behind me, and I feel her hand grasp the back of my shirt.

"Mike," she whispers, "what exactly did you see up here before?"

I hesitate, the memory of the shadowy figure sending a chill down my spine. "I'm not sure. But whatever it was, it felt... significant."

We reach the attic door, its weathered surface looming before us. My hand trembles slightly as I reach for the knob.

"Wait," Jake hisses, grabbing my wrist. "What if it's dangerous?"

I meet his worried gaze. "We have to know, Jake. For all of us."

Taking a deep breath, I turn the knob and push the door open. It creaks ominously, revealing the attic beyond. As we step inside, our phone lights dance across the space, illuminating years of forgotten relics and dust-covered memories.

But it's the walls that capture our attention. Etched into the aged wood, a series of intricate symbols spiral outward, covering nearly every surface. They seem to pulse with an otherworldly energy, drawing us closer.

"Holy shit," Tom breathes, his eyes wide. "What are these?"

I reach out, my fingers hovering just above one of the symbols. It feels warm, alive somehow. "I think... I think these are the trials," I whisper, a mix of awe and fear coursing through me.

Sarah moves to another section, her brow furrowed. "They're like nothing I've ever seen. Some kind of ancient language, maybe?"

As we examine the symbols, a strange sensation washes over me. It's as if the attic itself is alive, watching us, judging us. The air feels charged, electric.

"Guys," I say, my voice barely audible, "I think we've found what we've been looking for. Whatever these trials are, whatever we have to face... it all starts here."

The weight of my words hangs in the air, heavy and suffocating. I watch as my friends' faces contort with a mix of emotions - fear, doubt, and a glimmer of something that might be hope.

"Are you sure about this, Mike?" Sarah whispers, her voice trembling. "These symbols... they're not just creepy drawings. They feel... alive." She hugs herself, eyes darting nervously around the attic.

Tom runs a shaky hand through his hair. "I don't know if I can do this," he admits, his usual bravado crumbling. "What if we're not cut out for these trials? What if we make things worse?"

I feel their fear, their uncertainty. It mirrors my own, churning in my gut like a storm. But beneath it, something else stirs - a resolve I didn't know I had.

"We have to try," I say, my voice steadier than I feel. "For Jake. For all of us."

I turn to face my friends, taking in their anxious glances and hunched shoulders. "Look, I'm scared too. But we're in this together. Whatever these trials throw at us, we face it as a team."

As I speak, I feel a change within me. The fear is still there, but it's no longer paralyzing. Instead, it sharpens my focus, steeling my nerves.

"We've come too far to back down now," I continue, meeting each of their gazes. "We can do this. We have to."

I see a flicker of determination in Sarah's eyes, a slight straightening of Tom's shoulders. It's not much, but it's a start.

"So," I say, turning back to the symbols, "let's figure out what these mean. It's time we take control of this game."

I hold out my hand, palm down, in the center of our huddled group. "We're in this together," I say, my voice low but firm. "No matter what happens, we don't abandon each other. We face these trials as one."

Sarah's hand joins mine first, her fingers trembling slightly but her grip strong. "For Jake," she whispers, her eyes glistening with unshed tears.

Tom hesitates, his brow furrowed with doubt. But after a moment, he places his hand on top of ours. "I'm terrified," he admits, "but I'm with you guys."

Alex is the last to join, his usual sarcasm replaced by a solemn nod. "Let's show this game what we're made of," he says, a hint of his old bravado returning.

As our hands connect, I feel a surge of energy, like an electric current passing between us. It's more than just a pact; it's a promise, a bond forged in the face of the unknown.

"Whatever comes next," I say, looking at each of my friends in turn, "we face it together. No hesitation, no turning back."

We break apart, and I can see the change in their postures, the set of their jaws. The fear is still there, but it's tempered now by something stronger: determination.

As we turn back to the cryptic symbols on the attic walls, I can't shake the feeling that we've just crossed a threshold. Whatever these trials are, whatever dangers lie ahead, we're ready to face them.

The game may have started this, but we're going to finish it. Together.

CHAPTER 4

Trials of the Spirit

My heart pounds like a jackhammer as I stand before the looming entrance of the maze, its dark maw seeming to beckon me forward. I clench my fists, trying to still the trembling in my hands. This is it. No turning back now.

"You can do this, Mike," I whisper to myself, the words barely audible even in the oppressive silence. "One step at a time."

Taking a deep breath, I force my legs to move. The first step is always the hardest, but I've come too far to give up now. Fear gnaws at my insides like a hungry beast, but I push it down, focusing instead on the determination burning in my chest.

As I cross the threshold, the world around me shifts. The walls of the maze, once solid and imposing, begin to move and change. It's like watching a time-lapse of ivy growing, except these tendrils are made of stone and shadow.

"What the hell?" I mutter, spinning around to try and keep my bearings. But it's useless. The entrance has vanished, swallowed up by the ever-changing labyrinth.

My footsteps echo unnaturally loud in the eerie silence, each scuff of my sneakers against the ground sounding like a thunderclap. I can hear my own breathing, rapid and shallow, and the frantic beating of my heart.

"Stay calm," I tell myself, pressing a hand against the nearest wall to steady myself. "You've faced worse than this. Just keep moving forward."

But as I take another step, the maze shifts again. Walls that were once solid melt away like mist, while new barriers spring up in their place. It's disorienting, like trying to walk straight after spinning in circles.

I strain my ears, listening for any sound that might give me a clue, a direction to follow. But there's nothing. Just the deafening silence and the occasional scrape of stone on stone as the maze continues its ceaseless transformation.

"Okay, think," I say aloud, needing to hear a voice, even if it's just my own. "There has to be a pattern, a logic to this. I just need to figure it out."

But as I stand there, trying to make sense of the ever-changing landscape around me, I can't shake the feeling that I'm being watched. Observed. Judged.

I shake my head, trying to clear away the paranoia. "Focus, Mike. One step at a time. That's all you can do."

With a deep breath, I force myself to move forward once more, into the heart of the shifting maze. Whatever challenges lie ahead, I have to face them. It's the only way out. The only way forward.

As I round another corner, my breath catches in my throat. There, in the shadows, a figure takes shape. It's me, but not me. A darker version, all my insecurities given form.

"Look who's trying to be a grown-up," it sneers, its voice echoing off the maze walls. "You really think you're ready for the real world, Mikey?"

I freeze, my heart hammering against my ribs. "You're not real," I mutter, but my voice wavers.

The shadow laughs, a chilling sound. "I'm as real as your doubts, kid. You can't even decide what to have for breakfast without second-guessing yourself. How are you going to handle a job? Bills? Relationships?"

I clench my fists, trying to steady myself. "I... I'll figure it out," I say, but the words sound hollow even to me.

"Will you?" it taunts. "Or will you just keep running back to mommy and daddy every time things get tough?"

My mind races, memories of missed opportunities and small failures flooding in. That time I chickened out of asking Sarah to prom. The job interview I bombed last month.

"I'm not a kid anymore," I say, but it comes out as a whisper.

"Aren't you?" The shadow grows, looming over me. "Face it, Mike. You're in over your head. Always have been, always will be."

I take a step back, my resolve crumbling. How can I face the world when I can't even face myself?

I close my eyes, drawing in a deep breath. The shadow's words sting, but something inside me shifts. A spark of defiance ignites.

"No," I say, my voice stronger now. "You're wrong."

I open my eyes, squaring my shoulders. "I might not have all the answers, but who does? I'm not running anymore."

With a surge of determination, I take a decisive step forward, directly towards the looming shadow. "I'm facing you, and I'm facing my fears. That's what being an adult really means."

The shadow wavers, its form flickering. "Bold words, little Mikey. But can you back them up?"

"Watch me," I growl, pushing forward.

As I move, the maze around me groans and shifts. The walls ripple like water, reforming into a new configuration. The shadow dissipates, but the challenge isn't over.

Before me stretches a dizzying array of obstacles. Swinging pendulums, rotating platforms, and narrow ledges over seemingly bottomless pits.

"Great," I mutter, eyeing the treacherous path. "From mind games to an obstacle course. Because why not?"

I approach the first challenge - a series of platforms moving in erratic patterns. Timing is crucial.

"Okay, Mike," I tell myself, "it's just like that dancing game at the arcade. Rhythm and timing."

I watch the platforms, noting their patterns. One, two, three... I leap. My foot lands squarely on the first platform. No time to celebrate - I'm already eyeing the next jump.

As I navigate the course, ducking under swinging blades and leaping across chasms, I realize something. "I'm... actually doing this," I say between breaths. "I'm figuring it out as I go."

Maybe that's what being an adult really is - not having all the answers, but being willing to face the challenges head-on.

As I clear the last obstacle, my chest heaving from exertion, a familiar scene materializes before me. The maze walls fade, replaced by the dingy basement of Tyler's house. My stomach lurches as I recognize the moment.

"Come on, Mike, don't be such a wimp," Tyler's voice echoes, tinged with mockery. "It's just one hit. Everyone's doing it."

I watch my younger self, eyes darting nervously between the joint in Tyler's hand and the expectant faces of our so-called friends. The pressure is palpable, suffocating.

"No," I whisper, willing my past self to refuse. But I already know what happens.

My younger self reaches out with trembling fingers, takes the joint, and inhales deeply. The room erupts in cheers, but all I feel is a crushing wave of regret.

"God, I was so stupid," I mutter, running a hand through my hair. "I threw away months of training, let down my team, all because I couldn't say no to these jerks."

The scene fades, leaving me alone in the maze once more. But the weight of that decision lingers, heavy on my shoulders.

"Never again," I vow, clenching my fists. "I'm done letting others dictate my choices."

With renewed determination, I press forward. The maze, however, seems to have other plans. What was once a straightforward path now twists and turns unpredictably. Dead ends appear out of nowhere, forcing me to backtrack.

"Come on!" I growl in frustration, hitting another wall. "This is getting ridiculous."

I take a deep breath, trying to calm my racing thoughts. "Okay, Mike, think. There's got to be a pattern here."

I start paying closer attention to the subtle shifts in the walls, the barely perceptible changes in air currents. Slowly, a method to the madness emerges.

"Left, right, then two rights," I mutter, following my instincts. "It's like a combination lock, but with directions."

Despite the maze's best efforts to confuse me, I press on. Each correct turn fuels my determination. I may not have all the answers, but I'm learning, adapting. And right now, that's enough.

As I round another corner, the air suddenly grows thick and heavy. A chill runs down my spine, and I freeze in my tracks. There, in the shadows ahead, a figure materializes - but it's not like the others I've encountered. This one is achingly familiar.

"Mom?" I whisper, my voice cracking.

The figure turns, and I see her face - a perfect recreation of my mother's features, but twisted with disappointment and indifference. Her eyes, once warm and loving, now regard me with cold detachment.

"Mike," she says, her voice echoing unnaturally. "Why are you even trying? We both know you'll never measure up."

I stumble back, my chest tightening. "That's not true," I argue, but my voice sounds weak even to my own ears.

The apparition of my mother moves closer, its presence suffocating. "We left because we knew you'd fail. It was easier to start over without the burden of your mediocrity."

Tears sting my eyes, and I feel that old, familiar pain of abandonment washing over me. For a moment, I'm that scared little boy again, watching my family drive away without a backward glance.

"No," I mutter, shaking my head. "This isn't real. You're not real."

The figure sneers. "But the truth is, isn't it? Deep down, you know we were right to leave."

I close my eyes, trying to block out its words, but they seep into my mind like poison. Years of self-doubt and insecurity threaten to overwhelm me.

But then, a small voice in the back of my head speaks up. It's my own voice, but stronger, more assured.

"You're wrong," I say, opening my eyes to face the apparition. "I am not defined by your actions or your opinions of me."

The figure wavers, its certainty faltering.

"I've made it this far on my own," I continue, my voice growing stronger. "Every obstacle I've overcome, every challenge I've faced - that was all me. Not you, not anyone else."

I take a step forward, and the apparition retreats. "I may have been abandoned, but I'm not broken. I'm building my own path, my own family. And I don't need your approval to know my worth."

As I speak these words, I feel something shift inside me. The pain is still there, but it no longer controls me. I stand taller, my gaze steady.

"You have no power over me," I declare, my voice ringing with newfound confidence.

The apparition flickers, its form becoming less substantial with each passing second. As it fades away, I catch a glimpse of something in its eyes - not disappointment or indifference, but a fleeting look of pride.

And then it's gone, leaving me alone in the maze once more. But this time, I don't feel lonely. I feel... free.

I take a deep breath, feeling the weight of the moment settle around me. Suddenly, the maze begins to shift. The towering walls that once seemed impenetrable start to crumble, disintegrating like sand castles against the tide. I watch in awe as pathways open up before me, revealing a clearer route ahead.

"Is this... is this really happening?" I whisper to myself, my heart pounding with a mixture of relief and excitement.

As I take a tentative step forward, I feel a rush of accomplishment wash over me. It's as if the maze itself is acknowledging my progress, rewarding me for facing my demons head-on.

"I did it," I say, a smile tugging at the corners of my mouth. "I actually did it."

But even as I savor this moment of triumph, a nagging voice in the back of my mind reminds me that this is far from over. The maze may be unraveling, but I can sense more challenges lurking in the shadows ahead.

I find a relatively calm spot amidst the shifting landscape and sit down, leaning against a partially crumbled wall. It's time to take stock of what I've learned.

"Okay, Mike," I say to myself, closing my eyes. "What have you figured out so far?"

My mind races through the events of the past few hours - the fears I've faced, the doubts I've overcome. Each challenge has taught me something about myself, about my own strength and resilience.

"I'm not the same person who entered this maze," I realize aloud. "I'm stronger now. More... me."

I open my eyes, gazing at the ever-changing paths before me. "Facing my fears head-on... it's not easy, but it's necessary. It's the only way forward."

A memory flashes through my mind - the moment I stood up to the apparition of my family's abandonment. The fear I felt, the courage it took to confront it.

"That's the key," I mutter, getting to my feet. "No more running. No more hiding. Whatever this maze throws at me next, I'll face it. Because now I know I can."

With renewed determination, I step back onto the path, ready to tackle whatever comes next. The maze may not be finished with me yet, but I'm no longer the same Mike who entered it. I'm evolving, growing stronger with each step. And whatever lies ahead, I'll face it head-on.

As I round the next corner, my heart nearly stops. The path ahead suddenly drops away into a yawning chasm, impossibly wide and deep. Across the void, I can see the exit - tantalisingly close, yet unreachable.

"What the hell?" I mutter, my voice echoing in the vast space. "This... this can't be right."

I approach the edge cautiously, peering down into the darkness below. No bottom in sight. My mind races, trying to make sense of this new challenge.

"Okay, think Mike," I say to myself, running a hand through my hair. "There's got to be a way across. The maze wouldn't give me an impossible task... would it?"

As I scan the chasm, I notice something glinting in the dim light. Squinting, I can just make out a series of small, floating platforms - each no bigger than a dinner plate - suspended in mid-air across the void.

My stomach drops. "You've got to be kidding me."

For a moment, panic threatens to overwhelm me. How can I possibly cross on those tiny platforms? One misstep and I'd plummet into the abyss.

But then I take a deep breath, closing my eyes. I think back to everything I've faced in this maze - the shadows of my past, my fears of inadequacy, the specter of abandonment. I've overcome them all.

"I can do this," I say, opening my eyes with newfound determination. "I've come too far to give up now."

I step back, giving myself a running start. As I approach the edge, I steel myself for the leap.

"Here goes nothing," I mutter, and jump.

I land on the first platform with a wobble, arms pinwheeling to keep my balance. For a heart-stopping moment, I think I might fall, but I steady myself. One down, many more to go.

"Okay, Mike. You've got this," I whisper, eyeing the next platform. It's a good six feet away, and even smaller than the first.

I take a deep breath, bend my knees, and leap. My foot catches the edge, and I stumble forward, barely managing to stay upright. Sweat beads on my forehead as I look ahead at the remaining platforms. They seem to stretch endlessly into the darkness.

"Focus," I tell myself. "One at a time."

With each jump, I feel my confidence growing. My movements become more fluid, more assured. The fear is still there, churning in my gut, but it no longer paralyzes me. Instead, it sharpens my senses, keeps me alert.

As I near the end, I allow myself a small smile. "Almost there," I pant.

The final platform looms ahead, larger than the others. Beyond it, I can see solid ground. Freedom. With one last burst of energy, I launch myself forward.

I hit the platform hard, rolling to absorb the impact. As I stand, my legs shaking from exertion, I realize I've made it. The exit to the maze is just a few steps away.

Stumbling forward, I cross the threshold. The maze's oppressive atmosphere lifts, and I find myself in a small, circular room. A single door stands before me, unmarked and unassuming.

I pause, my hand on the doorknob. What lies beyond? More trials? The final confrontation?

"Whatever it is," I say aloud, my voice echoing in the empty space, "I'm ready."

With a deep breath, I turn the knob and step through, exhausted but triumphant, ready to face whatever comes next.

CHAPTER 5

The Cosmic Showdown

I stand at the edge of reality, my breath caught in my throat as I take in the surreal landscape before me. The air shimmers with an otherworldly energy, pulsing and twisting like a living thing. My heart pounds in my chest, a frantic rhythm that matches the swirling chaos around me.

"This is it," I whisper to myself, clenching my fists at my sides. "Everything has led to this moment."

I close my eyes for a brief second, allowing the memories of my journey to wash over me. The friends I've made, the challenges I've overcome, the growth I've experienced - it all comes rushing back, filling me with a sense of purpose.

Taking a deep breath, I open my eyes and step forward. The instant my foot touches the ground, the world shifts. The terrain beneath me warps and undulates, as if I'm walking on a living, breathing entity. I stumble, my arms flailing as I fight to keep my balance.

"Whoa!" I gasp, planting my feet wide. "Steady, Mike. You've come too far to fall now."

As I regain my footing, I force myself to focus. The stakes of this confrontation loom large in my mind - the fate of Jake, the stability of reality itself. I can't afford to be distracted by the mind-bending environment.

"Remember why you're here," I mutter, gritting my teeth as I take another careful step forward. "For Jake. For everyone back home. For the countless realities at risk."

The landscape continues to shift and change with each movement, a dizzying display of impossibility. Colors blend and separate, structures appear and disappear in the blink of an eye. It's like walking through a fever dream, but I press on, driven by determination.

"I've faced worse than this," I remind myself, thinking back to the trials I've endured. "I've outsmarted AI overlords, navigated time loops, and survived reality-bending puzzles. This is just another challenge to overcome."

As I push deeper into the chaotic realm, I can't help but feel a mix of awe and trepidation. The power required to create and maintain such a place is beyond comprehension. But I've learned that even the mightiest forces have their weaknesses, and I'm determined to find them.

"Alright, ChrotoQuest," I say aloud, my voice steady despite the fear churning in my gut. "Show me what you've got. I'm ready for whatever comes next."

With that declaration, I steel myself and continue forward, ready to face the creator of this mad multiverse and bring an end to their reality-warping game once and for all.

As I take another step, the swirling chaos before me parts like a curtain, revealing a figure that defies description. The creator of ChrotoQuest emerges from the shadows, their presence sending a chill down my spine.

Their form shifts constantly, at once solid and ethereal. One moment, they appear as a towering giant with skin like starry night; the next, a shimmering, humanoid vortex of energy. Eyes that could be galaxies or black holes regard me with an unsettling calmness.

"Mike," the creator speaks, their voice resonating from everywhere and nowhere at once. "You've come so far, only to fail at the final hurdle. How... predictably human."

I clench my fists, pushing down the fear threatening to overwhelm me. "I'm not here to fail," I retort, surprised by the strength in my own voice. "I'm here to end this madness and save my friend."

The creator's laughter echoes around me, a sound both beautiful and terrifying. "End it? You can't even comprehend it. Your mortal mind is but a speck in the vastness of what I've created."

I think of Jake, of Sarah and the others who've helped me along the way. Their faces flash through my mind, giving me strength. "Maybe I can't comprehend it all," I admit, "but I understand enough. I've learned, I've grown, and I'm not leaving without setting things right."

The creator's form coalesces into something vaguely humanoid, a smirk playing on features that seem to shift with every blink. "Your determination is admirable, if misguided. Tell me, Mike, what makes you think you can challenge a god?"

I stand my ground, drawing on every lesson, every victory that's brought me here. "Because I'm not alone," I say, my voice steady. "I carry the strength of everyone I've met, everyone I'm fighting for. And that's something even you can't take away."

The creator's eyes flash with an otherworldly light, and suddenly the world around me warps. I'm no longer standing on solid ground, but floating in a vast, starry void. Planets and galaxies swirl around me, each one a potential reality.

"Let's see how well you've learned, shall we?" The creator's voice booms from everywhere and nowhere.

Before I can respond, I'm plummeting through the void. Terror grips me as I fall, but I force myself to focus. This isn't real, I remind myself. It's just another illusion.

I close my eyes, concentrating on the feeling of solid ground beneath my feet. When I open them again, I'm standing in a familiar place – my childhood bedroom. But something's off. The shadows are too long, too dark.

"Remember this?" The creator's voice whispers. "The night terrors that kept you awake? The monsters under your bed?"

The shadows start to move, taking on grotesque shapes. I feel my heart racing, that old, primal fear threatening to take over. But I stand my ground.

"I'm not that scared little boy anymore," I say, my voice shaking only slightly. "I've faced my fears head-on in this game. They don't control me."

The shadows recede, but the room starts to spin. Walls become floors, ceilings become walls. I stumble, trying to keep my balance in this twisted version of M.C. Escher's nightmares.

"Impressive," the creator muses. "But how will you fare when the very fabric of reality turns against you?"

The room explodes outward, reforming into an endless maze of staircases and doorways. I can see glimpses of other realities through some of the doors – worlds where history took different turns, where the laws of physics don't apply.

I take a deep breath, calming my racing thoughts. "You're trying to disorient me," I say, more to myself than the creator. "But I've navigated trickier puzzles than this."

I start moving, letting my instincts guide me. Left turn here, right turn there. I ignore the dizzying drops and impossible angles, focusing instead on the subtle clues – a familiar scent, a flash of color that feels right.

"Your resilience is admirable," the creator's voice echoes. "But how long can you keep this up?"

I grit my teeth, pushing forward. "As long as it takes," I mutter. "I didn't come this far to give up now."

I find a moment of respite in a pocket of calm amidst the chaos. Leaning against a wall that feels solid – for now – I catch my breath and reflect on how far I've come.

"Jake," I whisper, his name a talisman against the madness. "I'm coming for you, buddy."

The qualities I've honed throughout this journey flash through my mind: courage in the face of my deepest fears, adaptability in ever-changing landscapes, and an unwavering determination that's carried me this far.

"I've changed," I realize aloud. "This game... it's made me stronger."

The creator's voice slithers through the air. "Touching. But strength alone won't save you or your friend."

I straighten up, a newfound resolve steeling my nerves. "Maybe not. But I've got more than just strength on my side."

The world twists again, more violently this time. Colors bleed and blur, gravity shifts unpredictably. I'm falling, flying, spinning – sometimes all at once.

"Let's see how your loyalty fares when you can't tell up from down," the creator taunts.

I close my eyes, focusing on the faces of my friends. Jake's goofy grin, Sarah's determined eyes, even Kevin's annoying smirk. They ground me, anchoring my sense of self in this maelstrom.

"My friends are my compass," I shout, opening my eyes to face whatever comes next. "And they're pointing me straight to you!"

The creator's laughter echoes, bone-chilling and distorted. Suddenly, the chaos coalesces into a scene that makes my blood run cold. I'm standing in my childhood bedroom, but it's warped, twisted into a nightmarish parody.

"Let's see how your self-acceptance fares against the demons you've buried, Mike," the creator's voice hisses.

From the shadows, figures emerge – manifestations of my deepest insecurities and fears. There's the hulking form of my childhood bully, sneering and cracking his knuckles. Beside him, a disappointed version of my father shakes his head, muttering about wasted potential. And in the corner, a grotesque representation of my own self-doubt writhes and whispers poisonous thoughts.

"You're nothing," the bully growls, advancing. "Just a scared little boy playing hero."

I feel my resolve wavering, old wounds threatening to reopen. But then I remember everything I've overcome to get here.

"No," I say, my voice gaining strength. "I'm not that kid anymore. I've faced my fears, I've grown."

I turn to face the apparition of my father. "I've made my own path, and I'm proud of who I've become."

The disappointed figure begins to fade, and I feel a weight lift from my shoulders.

The self-doubt creature shrieks, "You'll fail! You always do!"

I take a deep breath, centering myself. "I might fail," I admit. "But I'll keep trying. That's who I am now."

With each confrontation, the room starts to fracture, reality breaking apart at the seams. As my demons dissolve, I notice glowing shards floating in the air – pieces of the world itself.

"This is it," I realize aloud. "The key to beating the game, to saving Jake – it's putting reality back together!"

I reach out, grabbing a fragment. It hums with energy, and I instinctively know where it belongs. As I start piecing the shards together, I can feel the creator's fury building.

"You think you can mend what I've broken?" they roar.

I grit my teeth, focusing on the task at hand. "Watch me."

The creator's rage manifests as a tempest of swirling colors and distorted shapes, threatening to tear apart the very fabric of existence. I feel the assault on every level of my being – my body, my mind, my soul. It's as if reality itself is trying to reject me.

"You're nothing!" the creator's voice booms, seeming to come from everywhere at once. "A speck of dust in the vastness of the multiverse!"

I grit my teeth, forcing myself to keep working. My hands tremble as I fit another shard into place. "Maybe," I grunt, "but this speck isn't giving up."

The pressure intensifies, and I feel like I'm being crushed from all sides. My vision blurs, and for a moment, I lose my grip on the fragments. No, I can't fail now. Jake is counting on me. Everyone is.

"You can't win," the creator taunts. "I am the architect of realities!"

I close my eyes, centering myself. "And I," I say, my voice barely a whisper, "am the one who's going to fix what you've broken."

With renewed determination, I push through the pain. Each piece I connect feels like a small victory. The landscape around us starts to stabilize, colors becoming more vivid, shapes more defined.

"Impossible!" the creator screams, their voice tinged with fear for the first time.

I allow myself a small smile. "Nothing's impossible. That's what this journey has taught me."

As I slot the final piece into place, there's a blinding flash of light. When it fades, I find myself standing on solid ground. The chaotic maelstrom is gone, replaced by a serene, albeit strange, landscape.

The creator stands before me, their form no longer shifting and unstable. They look... diminished.

"How?" they ask, their voice a mixture of awe and frustration. "How did you do it?"

I meet their gaze, steady and unafraid. "By remembering who I am, and what really matters."

The creator nods slowly, a grudging respect in their eyes. "Perhaps... perhaps I underestimated the power of human determination."

I feel the weight of my journey settling onto my shoulders, but for the first time, it doesn't feel like a burden. It feels like strength.

I take a deep breath, feeling the enormity of what I've accomplished wash over me. The air around me feels different now - cleaner, more real. I look down at my hands, marveling at how they no longer shimmer with uncertainty.

"I did it," I whisper, more to myself than anyone else. "I actually did it."

The creator, now a shadow of their former self, watches me with curiosity. "You've changed, Mike," they observe. "You're not the same person who stumbled into ChrotoQuest."

I nod, feeling a surge of emotions. "You're right. I'm not."

As I stand there, memories of my journey flash through my mind - the fears I've faced, the challenges I've overcome. Each one has left its mark, shaping me into someone stronger, wiser.

"I came here looking for Jake," I say, my voice steady. "But I found myself along the way."

The creator tilts their head. "And was it worth it?"

I pause, considering. "Every moment," I finally reply. "Even the painful ones."

I close my eyes, feeling the pull of my own reality calling me back. It's time to go home, but I know I'm not leaving empty-handed.

"The game is over," I say, opening my eyes. "But the lessons... those are mine to keep."

As the world around me begins to fade, I can't help but smile. ChrotoQuest may be ending, but my real adventure is just beginning.

CHAPTER 6

The Price of Freedom

The air crackles with electricity as I stand face-to-face with the creator of ChronoQuest. My heart pounds, but I force myself to stand tall. The figure before me is both terrifying and mesmerizing - a swirling vortex of cosmic energy barely contained in human form.

"So, you've made it to the final level," the creator says, their voice echoing from everywhere and nowhere. "I'm almost impressed."

I clench my fists, drawing on every ounce of courage I've gained through countless time loops. "This ends now. I won't let you keep torturing people for your sick game."

The creator laughs, the sound sending chills down my spine. "You think you can stop me? I am a god in this realm!"

Suddenly, the world around us begins to warp and twist. Buildings bend like rubber, the sky fractures like shattered glass. I stumble, fighting waves of vertigo.

No. I can't let them get in my head. I close my eyes, remembering all the skills I've honed, all the lessons I've learned.

"Nice try," I growl, planting my feet firmly. "But I've seen worse. You'll have to do better than that."

The creator's eyes narrow. "Very well."

The air shimmers, and suddenly I'm surrounded by copies of myself - hundreds of Mikes from different timelines. But I know this trick. I've faced my own demons before.

"I'm the real me," I declare, my voice steady. "The one who's going to end this."

One by one, the copies fade away. The creator's confident smirk falters for just a moment.

I press my advantage. "You may control this world, but you don't control me. Not anymore."

As I speak, I feel a surge of power within me - the culmination of every choice, every failure, every tiny victory that's led me to this moment. I am more than just a player in their game now.

The creator's form flickers, their confidence clearly shaken. "Impossible. You're just a human, a pawn-"

"I'm the one who's going to set everyone free," I interrupt, taking a step forward. "Including you."

As I take another step toward the creator, a sudden realization hits me like a punch to the gut. Jake. In all this chaos, I'd almost forgotten why I started this journey in the first place.

"Wait," I whisper, my voice barely audible. The creator pauses, curiosity gleaming in their otherworldly eyes.

I swallow hard, my throat tight. "Jake. What happens to him if I end this?"

The creator's lips curl into a cruel smile. "Your friend? He's part of the game now. End it, and you end him too."

My heart plummets. "No," I breathe. "There has to be another way."

"Mike?" Jake's voice echoes from somewhere beyond, faint and distant. "Mike, help me!"

I close my eyes, memories flooding back. Jake and I, laughing over stupid jokes. Late-night gaming sessions. The way he always had my back, no matter what.

"What'll it be, Mike?" the creator taunts. "Save the world, or save your friend?"

My fists clench at my sides. "Both," I growl. "I'm going to save both."

The creator laughs. "Impossible. Unless..."

"Unless what?" I demand.

Their eyes lock onto mine. "Unless you're willing to make a sacrifice. A piece of yourself, for his freedom."

I don't hesitate. "Done."

"Mike, no!" Jake's voice cries out.

"It's okay, buddy," I say softly. "I've got this."

I turn to the creator. "What do I have to do?"

They gesture, and a shimmering portal appears. "Step through. Give up a part of your essence. Your friend goes free, but you... well, you won't be quite the same."

I take a deep breath, steeling myself. This is it. The moment everything has been leading to.

"Mike, please," Jake pleads. "Don't do this."

I smile, even though he can't see me. "Sorry, Jake. But that's what friends are for."

With one last look at the creator, I step into the portal. Pain explodes through every fiber of my being. It feels like I'm being torn apart, molecule by molecule. Memories flash before my eyes - childhood, family, Jake, the loops - all blurring together.

I scream, but no sound comes out. My vision goes white, then black. I'm falling, dissolving, becoming something else entirely.

Through it all, one thought keeps me anchored: Jake will be safe. It's worth it. It has to be.

As consciousness starts to slip away, I hear Jake's voice one last time: "Mike! I'll find you, I swear!"

Then, nothing.

The world shatters.

There's no other way to describe it. Reality cracks like glass, splintering into a million shimmering shards. Each fragment holds a piece of a timeline, a snapshot of a world I've lived through. I see myself dying, living, laughing, crying—all at once.

"What's happening?" I try to shout, but my voice is lost in the cacophony of breaking universes.

The air itself seems to vibrate, humming with discordant energy. Colors bleed and swirl, defying logic. Up becomes down, left becomes right. I'm falling, floating, spinning—all simultaneously.

Through the chaos, I catch glimpses of Jake. He's screaming, reaching for me, but he's getting further away with each passing second.

"Jake!" I call out, stretching my hand towards him. But it's futile. He's fading, becoming just another fractured piece of the collapsing multiverse.

The noise is deafening—a symphony of destruction as every timeline I've experienced collapses in on itself. It's beautiful and terrifying, like watching a supernova from the inside.

And then, abruptly, silence.

The transition is so sudden it's disorienting. One moment, I'm in the eye of a reality storm. The next, I'm... nowhere.

I blink, trying to make sense of my surroundings. But there are no surroundings. Just... nothingness. An endless void stretches in every direction, featureless and dark.

"Hello?" I call out, my voice sounding small and muffled. There's no echo, no response. Just a oppressive, suffocating quiet.

I try to move, but there's no sense of up or down, no reference point. Am I floating? Standing? I can't tell.

"Jake?" I whisper, a creeping dread settling in my stomach. "Anyone?"

But I know, with a certainty that chills me to my core, that I'm utterly alone.

The silence presses in, a stark contrast to the chaos of moments before. It's almost tangible, wrapping around me like a smothering blanket.

I close my eyes, trying to center myself. "Think, Mike," I mutter. "What happened? Where are you?"

But my thoughts feel sluggish, disconnected. Did the sacrifice work? Is Jake safe? Am I... dead?

The questions swirl in my mind, finding no purchase in this featureless void. I've never felt so lost, so utterly untethered from reality.

And yet, beneath the fear and confusion, there's a glimmer of something else. A sense that, somehow, this isn't the end. That there's still more to come.

I take a deep breath—or at least, I think I do. In this strange non-place, even that simple act feels uncertain.

"Okay," I say to the endless nothing. "What's next?"

I blink, and suddenly there's light filtering through my eyelids. The void dissolves, replaced by the soft glow of morning sunlight. I'm lying on something soft, familiar. My bed?

My eyes flutter open, squinting against the brightness. The popcorn ceiling of my bedroom comes into focus, each tiny bump a comforting landmark. I inhale deeply, catching the faint scent of laundry detergent from my sheets and the lingering aroma of last night's pizza.

"What the..." I mutter, pushing myself up on my elbows. My alarm clock blinks 7:15 AM in angry red digits. The steady tick-tock of the wall clock feels almost deafening after the absolute silence of the void.

I swing my legs over the side of the bed, my feet connecting with the cool hardwood floor. Everything looks normal, painfully ordinary. My cluttered desk, the faded posters on the walls, even the pile of dirty clothes in the corner.

"Was it all a dream?" I wonder aloud, rubbing my temples. But the memories feel too vivid, too real. The time loops, the cosmic showdown, Jake...

My heart clenches. "Jake," I whisper, scanning the room as if expecting to see him materialize.

I stumble to the window, yanking open the curtains. The street below is quiet, a few early morning joggers and dog-walkers going about their routines. No sign of reality fracturing, no hint of the chaos I'd just experienced.

"It's over," I realize, the words catching in my throat. "It's really over."

A wave of relief washes over me, so intense it makes my knees weak. But it's quickly followed by a hollowness in my chest, an ache I can't quite place.

"I made it back," I say to the empty room, trying to make sense of it all. "But at what cost?"

I stand there, staring out the window, watching as the world wakes up. It's surreal how everything can look so normal when I feel so fundamentally changed.

"I'm not the same person I was yesterday," I murmur, studying my reflection in the glass. The face looking back at me is familiar, but the eyes... they hold a depth I've never seen before.

I take a deep breath, feeling a newfound strength coursing through my veins. "I survived," I say, my voice growing stronger. "I faced my worst fears, I pushed through when everything seemed hopeless. I... I beat the game."

A small, bitter laugh escapes me. "Some game."

I turn away from the window, my gaze falling on the photo of Jake and me on my nightstand. My throat tightens as I pick it up, tracing Jake's frozen smile with my finger.

"I wish you were here, man," I say, my voice cracking. "You'd probably say something stupid like, 'Dude, you totally leveled up!' And you'd be right."

The silence that follows is deafening. I've never felt Jake's absence more acutely than in this moment.

"I did it for you," I whisper, clutching the frame to my chest. "I hope... I hope it was worth it."

Tears sting my eyes, but I blink them back. "I won't let your sacrifice be in vain, Jake. I promise."

I set the photo back down, my hand lingering on it for a moment. "I'm going to live for both of us now. I'm going to make it count."

As I stare at Jake's photo, a sudden realization washes over me like a tidal wave. My mind reels, struggling to process the enormity of what I've experienced.

"Holy shit," I breathe, running a hand through my hair. "It wasn't just a game, was it? All those loops, all those different versions of reality..."

I pace the room, my thoughts racing. "The multiverse. It's real. Every choice, every possibility... they all exist simultaneously."

I turn to Jake's photo, as if he could confirm my revelation. "Remember when we used to argue about parallel universes? You always said they were just sci-fi nonsense."

A bittersweet smile tugs at my lips. "Guess you owe me five bucks, buddy."

The weight of this knowledge settles on my shoulders, both exhilarating and terrifying. I sink onto my bed, overwhelmed.

"So what does that make us?" I wonder aloud. "Are we just one version among infinite others? Or does that make our choices even more significant?"

THE ENDLESS GAME

I close my eyes, remembering the countless iterations I lived through. "Each decision, each moment... they all matter. They all create new realities."

Opening my eyes, I look at Jake's photo once more. "You're out there somewhere, aren't you? In another reality, we're probably still playing video games and arguing about stupid theories."

I stand up, a new resolve burning in my chest. "I can't change what happened here, but I can honor your memory. I can live the life you'd want me to live."

Walking to my desk, I pull out a notebook and a pen. "Starting now, I'm going to make every day count. For both of us."

I begin to write, my hand moving with purpose. "Jake, I promise I'll live with the courage you showed. I'll face each day as if it's a new level, a new chance to make a difference."

As I write, I feel a sense of peace settling over me. The pain of loss is still there, but it's tempered by a newfound strength and purpose.

"Thank you, Jake," I whisper, looking up from my writing. "For everything. I won't let you down."

As I set down my pen, a strange sensation washes over me. The air in my room seems to shimmer, like heat waves on a summer road. I blink, wondering if my eyes are playing tricks on me.

"What the..." I mutter, reaching out to touch the wavering space in front of me.

My fingertips brush against something that feels like static electricity, and suddenly, the world around me expands. It's as if I'm looking through a kaleidoscope of infinite possibilities, each one a different version of reality.

"Holy crap," I breathe, my heart racing. "Is this... are these all different universes?"

I see flashes of other lives, other versions of myself. In one, I'm a famous video game designer. In another, I'm exploring alien worlds. And in yet another, Jake and I are laughing together, oblivious to the trials we faced in this reality.

The visions fade as quickly as they appeared, leaving me breathless and dizzy. I stumble back, collapsing onto my bed.

"Was that real?" I wonder aloud, running a hand through my hair. "Or am I finally losing it?"

I close my eyes, trying to make sense of what I just experienced. When I open them again, my room looks normal, but something feels different. It's as if the air is charged with potential.

Standing up, I walk to my window and look out at the night sky. The stars seem brighter somehow, more alive.

"Maybe we're all part of something bigger," I whisper, pressing my hand against the cool glass. "A cosmic game of chance and choice, playing out across infinite realities."

I turn back to my room, my gaze falling on the notebook where I'd written my promise to Jake. A smile tugs at my lips.

"Guess I'd better make this playthrough count, huh?" I say to the empty room. "Who knows what levels are still ahead?"

As I settle back at my desk, ready to continue writing, I can't shake the feeling that I've glimpsed something profound. My story, Jake's story, they're just threads in an impossibly vast tapestry of existence.

And yet, somehow, that makes each thread all the more precious.

About the Author

Mortaza Tokhy is a child author with an astounding gift; At the tender age of twelve, he holds the title of the youngest published horror fiction author. With astonishing skill and creativity, Mortaza has crafted diabolically thrilling tales of paranormal, sci-fi and horror that captivates readers around the world. His razor sharp writing leaves many mouths agape in disbelief that someone so young could be capable of such works.

Read more at https://www.horrorvhorror.com/.

About the Publisher

As a boutique book publisher, we take on only a few new authors per year. We focus on building an author's brand, thereby directing more resources towards their overall success. Authors accepted by True American Publishing become creative partners, therefore, participating in their own success.